Quest FOR THE Keys

LEGO and the LEGO logo are trademarks of The LEGO Group. © 2015 The LEGO Group. Produced by Scholastic Inc. under license from The LEGO Group.

This book is a work of fiction. Names, characters, places, and incidents are either the product of the author's imagination or are used fictitiously, and any resemblance to actual persons, living or dead, business establishments, events, or locales is entirely coincidental.

ISBN 978-0-545-85280-7

10 9 8 7 6 5 4 3 2 1   15 16 17 18 19 20/0

Printed in the U.S.A.   40
First printing 2015

Book design by Angela Jun

Chapter 1

A Walk in the Garden

"Grandma wanted you to have this, Emily." Mrs. Jones sat down beside her daughter on the sofa. She opened her hand to reveal a large pendant hanging on a silver chain.

Emily Jones stared at the dark blue medallion and felt like there was a giant hole growing in her heart. Taking the necklace would mean that her grandmother was actually gone.

Though she knew it was impossible, Emily

kept imagining that Grandmother was going to walk into the living room at any second, tall and strong, and ask if Emily wanted to go on an adventure.

The heavy pendant swung from the chain in her mother's hand. Emily reached out toward it, then hesitated.

"Go on. Wear it," her father urged. "That way, she'll always be close."

Emily nodded. "Okay."

When her mother slipped the chain around her neck, the medallion felt cool and comforting. Emily touched it gently, then hugged her mom tight. Tears pressed against the back of her eyes even though she'd cried so much already.

"I miss her, too, honey." Mrs. Jones gave Emily a soft kiss on the forehead. "Your father and I have a few things to arrange. Would you like to spend some time in the garden?"

"Yes," Emily said. She had always felt closest to Grandmother in her garden. That was where they went on those "adventures," walking together for hours.

"Just a short walk today, okay?" her father said. "It'll start getting dark soon, and we're going to make dinner as soon as Mom and I finish with this."

"I won't go very far," Emily promised. The garden was huge and seemed to go on forever. Emily knew, even in all her visits, she'd never explored it all.

She started down the familiar trail, winding her way through flowers and trees. The heaviness around her heart lifted a little, and Emily wrapped her fingers tightly around her grandmother's medallion, and thought back to her childhood . . .

Emily was very young when she'd first noticed Grandmother's blue medallion. They were walking the garden path and Emily asked, "Where'd you get that? It's pretty."

Grandmother smiled, replying softly, "I've had it for a long, long time." She let her hands fall to her waist and turned Emily's attention to a nearby flower.

Grandmother would often point out plants, or sometimes small caves and animal burrows. Emily's parents were scientists, and they'd taught her the scientific name of many plants, but Grandmother had nicknames for everything, and stories about them. Of course, they were made up, but Grandmother made them seem so real. She told tales about plants that magical squirrels used for hats, tall trees where giants hid, and thorny bushes that elves crushed for medicine. Emily adored every story.

Her favorite flowers were the snapdragons (official name: Antirrhinum). She remembered the first time Grandmother showed her one.

"See how it looks like the face of a dragon?" Grandmother had asked. "If you gently pinch the sides of the flower, like this, the dragon's mouth opens wide!" Emily was surprised by how the blossom had almost looked like it came alive—like it really was a dragon's jaw.

Grandmother continued, "Dragons get mean when they are hungry, so be sure to feed them treats and keep their tummies full! I hear they like cookies." She smiled down at Emily. Emily wasn't sure if

Grandmother was serious or not, but she responded,
"I like cookies, too!"

Emily blinked in the afternoon sunlight and stepped over a broken tree branch. Suddenly, an owl zipped past, landing in a small tree nearby. Emily squinted at it. Grandmother had loved owls, and called the birds "hearts" because of the shape of their faces.

"Snowy owls don't have gold coloring on their chests," she told herself. Still, the bird's strange markings looked golden to her—almost like it was wearing jewelry. Even weirder, Emily was sure she'd seen this owl before . . .

One morning, after cutting through a thick, shadowed part of the garden, Emily swore she saw her grandmother up ahead talking to a small owl with a bright golden mark below its neck. Grandmother leaned close and whispered quietly, then cupped her ear as if to listen to a reply.

When the owl fluttered away, Emily didn't hesitate. She asked, "What did it say?"

Grandmother didn't answer right away, but clutched her medallion to her chest. Finally, she said, "Never forget, Emily, the heart knows the way."

That was a long time ago. She remembered excitedly telling her parents about it, but they had assured her that what she'd seen was impossible. Owls didn't talk to people. And Grandmother couldn't talk to owls. They had a hundred scientific reasons why it was unlikely that the bird Emily had seen was even an owl at all. Owls were nocturnal. They didn't like this climate. Plus, white owls didn't have strange golden markings.

But now, Emily was one hundred percent certain—this owl was real! It lifted its wings and floated on a breeze. The white feathers seemed to sparkle. This was crazy!

"I'm going to follow you," Emily declared. "That's what Grandmother would have done." Filled with confidence, she left the path and walked deeper into the overgrown garden as the owl soared ahead.

Emily noticed that the medallion around her neck had begun to feel warm, and when she looked down, it seemed to glow. As she neared a large oak tree in the center of the garden, the pendant lit up completely! It transformed into the deepest, most brilliant blue Emily had ever seen—the color of the afternoon sky on a clear summer day. It glittered and twinkled.

And then, a swirling, shimmering mist formed at the base of the oak tree. It completely covered the trunk behind it. A round blue opening seemed to form in the center of the swirl.

As Emily watched, the owl flew straight into the mist, through the opening—and disappeared.

"Whoa . . ." Stunned, she took a step back. What was she seeing? Was it just a patch of strange fog? Where had the owl gone?

Emily looked down at the glowing medallion, and then back toward her grandmother's house. The rest of the garden seemed perfectly normal—quiet and serene. Should she go back home?

The mist continued to swirl at the base of the oak tree. Emily closed her eyes. *The heart knows the way.* She took a step forward, and then another . . .

Chapter 2

Elvendale

"Wow!" Emily wasn't sure that what she was seeing was real. Before she knew it, she seemed to have gone through the oak tree . . . and now she was in another place entirely! The colors surrounding her were amazing. Red flowers looked redder. Green moss was greener. The blue sky was bluer. Emily blinked hard to make sure her eyes weren't playing tricks on her. They weren't. Grandmother would've loved to see this!

She took a good look around, and found she was in a forest of tall trees that stretched on as far as she could see.

This was definitely not her grandmother's garden! There were a lot of plants that Emily couldn't recognize. The sun was high in the sky, as if it were day and not evening. Nothing looked even a little familiar.

This was incredible.

This was *impossible*!

How could she have ended up in an entirely different forest?

"I have to show Mom and Dad!" she exclaimed.

But when she turned back toward the oak tree, the trunk was solid. There was no passageway.

"Oh no!"

Emily tried hard not to panic. She looked down at her grandmother's medallion. It was dull blue and cold, just like when her mother had given it to her.

"Stay calm," she told herself. "There has to be another way back to the house." She took a few steps backward as she searched for a path.

"*AAAH!*" she screamed when she bumped into something.

"*AAAH!*" a red-haired girl screamed back as they leapt away from each other. "Who are you?!"

Emily moved a safe distance away. She didn't know if she should stay or run away. She crossed her arms protectively over her chest and looked over at the girl. Emily had never seen anyone like her before. This girl had oddly pointed ears, fiery hair, and an unusual dress. The fabric sparkled like golden flames.

The girl appeared just as wary of Emily and was studying her intently.

Emily looked around the area in case she needed to escape. "I . . . I'm Emily Jones. Who are you? And where am I?"

"Whoa. One question at a time, Emily Jones," the girl said. She seemed to have decided Emily was safe. Her eyes flashed brightly. "There's no need to be afraid! I'm Azari, a fire elf, and you're in Elvendale."

Emily paused, staring hard at the girl. "A fire elf?" She was very confused. "What is that?"

"Hmmm . . ." Azari said with a silvery laugh. She walked in a big circle around Emily, studying her like a science project. "Curious," she muttered. "Very interesting . . ."

Emily held her breath as Azari got right in her face . . . and poked her in the nose.

"Hey!" cried Emily, cupping her nose with her hand. "That hurt."

Azari giggled. Her laughter sounded like tinkling bells. "I've heard stories about creatures like you," Azari said. "I just didn't believe they were true!" She pursed her lips and rubbed her chin thoughtfully. "So I'm gonna guess you're *not-an-elf*." She reached forward and pushed back Emily's long brown braid to get a better view of the side of her head. "I mean, those ears—wow!"

Emily quickly pulled her braid back. "What about *your* ears!" she exclaimed. "They're pointy, like something out of a comic book!"

"What's a comic book?" Azari asked, wrinkling her forehead. "Is that a good thing?"

"Um . . . yes." Emily gave a small nod. "It's a very good thing."

"Oh, how exciting! Wait till I tell the others!" Azari clapped. "I'm a comic book!"

Emily smiled and was about to explain, but decided it was just too complicated.

Azari looped her arm around Emily's shoulder. "I like you, Little Ears Emily. Welcome to Elvendale!" She started to lead her down a narrow path in the trees. "Come on. Let's go!"

"But, I—wait!" Emily's throat felt tight.

Azari stopped. "What's wrong?"

Emily glanced back toward the tree. "I can't go with you. I need to get home."

"Home? Where's that?" Azari asked.

"I somehow came through that tree." Emily sighed. "I was in my grandmother's garden, and suddenly this swirling doorway opened . . ."

Emily realized what had happened. "I guess it was a portal," she said, "and I went through it."

"A portal?" Azari asked.

"A passageway," Emily explained. "Like a tunnel to another place or time."

"A tunnel in the tree!" Azari dashed past Emily and pressed on the tree trunk. "How does it open?"

"I don't know," Emily admitted with a frown. "I wish I did."

"Stand back," Azari told Emily. The elf quickly cleared a circle of dirt and started a small fire on the ground. Her hands began to glow red, and then she used them to scoop up a ball of fire and throw it at the tree.

"What—?" Emily gasped.

"Open!" Azari commanded the tree. She threw another ball of flame. "Portal to the other world, open now!" The bark of the tree didn't change or move. Azari added, "Please!" but the portal stayed closed.

With a heavy moan, Emily said softly, "I'm lost."

"Lost . . ." Azari echoed. She sat silently for a beat, then jumped up. "Well, then, I know exactly what to do!" She took Emily's hand in hers. "We'll go see Farran!"

"Who's Farran?"

Azari didn't answer. The fire elf kept a tight grip on Emily's hand and moved fast. Emily had to jog to keep from tripping over thick tree roots as they hurried deeper into Elvendale— and farther away from the tree in the center of Grandmother's garden. Would she be stuck in Elvendale forever?

Chapter 3

A Way Back Home

"Who's Farran?" Emily asked again, out of breath, as they burst through a large cluster of trees onto a lush, flowering meadow.

There was a boy in a green outfit kneeling in the wild flowers right in front of them, but Azari didn't see him until it was too late. She hit him hard and stumbled, knocking all three of them over to the ground.

The boy leaned up on one arm, pushed a long strand of dark hair off his forehead, and grinned at Emily with twinkling green eyes. "You found me. I'm Farran."

"Oh," Emily said, surprised and embarrassed, as they stood up and brushed themselves off. It was an awkward way to meet the guy who might be able to help.

"Sorry about that," Azari said, picking a flower bloom out of his hair.

"That's okay. You're just bringing me closer to the earth I love!" Farran said with a smile. He picked up a few acorns off the ground and wiggled his fingers over them. The acorns quivered, then sprouted. "One day, Azari, you're going to startle me so bad, I'll step on these guys," he said.

"You and your acorn friends!" Azari laughed, then introduced Emily by saying, "Farran, meet

Emily Jones. She is not-an-elf." To prove it, she reached forward and pulled back Emily's hair so Farran could see her ears.

"Nice to meet—" He cut himself off when he got a good look at them. "Weird! Can I touch them? I've never seen anything like—"

Emily quickly pulled away, brushing her hair forward. As if she was the one with the weird ears!

"Sorry," Farran said with a deep chuckle. Emily thought it was a friendly laugh.

"No time for chitchat. We're in a hurry!" Azari explained about the portal in the tree. "Little Ears Emily needs our help."

"Ah," Farran said thoughtfully. "I see." He said to Emily, "You've come to the right place. I am an earth elf, and an expert at returning lost things to their homes." He started to tell her a story. "One time, there was a yellow-bellied bird who couldn't find her nest in a thick forest of trees, and I—"

"Farran!" Azari interrupted. "Emily's tree portal just closed."

"Right!" He rushed off, calling over his shoulder, "I'm going to need a few things."

Emily could hear Farran listing off the things he was gathering. "Shovel, pick, axe, spade, gloves . . ." They were all gardening tools.

While he was busy, Emily took a look around the meadow. She was surrounded by flowers in a rainbow of colors. She recognized a few from Grandmother's garden: lilies, roses, snap-dragons . . . But there were also flowers she'd never seen before, like ones with big yellow-orange blooms that drooped heavily, and strange square blossoms the color of ripe purple grapes. She saw a chipmunk scurry through the grass, and was certain she'd find some unfamiliar creatures if she had time to explore.

A wave of sadness swept over Emily, and she reached for her blue pendant. Grandmother would have loved it here. Emily wished they could have shared this adventure together.

"All right!" Farran said as he reappeared, carrying a large, clanking knapsack. "Let's see that tree of yours. I'll just use a little earth-elf magic, and . . ." He paused and turned toward Azari. "Well, I've actually never opened a portal before. Maybe we should call Aira, too, since she—"

"Way ahead of you, Farran!" Azari said, "I already tweeted."

"Tweeted?" Emily asked.

"You know, sending a message with a bird?" Azari replied. "Here's Aira now!" An elf with wild, long, flowing lavender hair—and matching dress—flew into the meadow, flapping a wide set of wings. As she landed, a gust of wind fluttered all the flowers in the meadow.

Now that this elf was closer, Emily could see that her wings were actually some kind of mechanical contraption strapped to her back. Interesting.

As Farran greeted Aira, Emily saw him blush.

"Hey!" Aira said, giving him a quick hug. "Pluma gave me Azari's message." She pointed to a small bird that was flying away. Then, she turned to Emily. "I can't wait to meet this not-an-elf!" She reached out and brushed back Emily's hair so fast, Emily didn't have time to resist. It felt like wind had pushed her braid back. "Cute round ears!" Aira exclaimed.

Emily gave up trying to cover them, instead taking the compliment. "Uh, thanks," she said.

"I'm Aira. I've come to help. Azari told me you have a big problem."

"Are you a wind elf?" Emily guessed.

"Exactly!" Aira smiled, taking off her wings and laying them nearby. "I hear you are trying to get home. Where's home?"

Emily wasn't sure how to answer. "I guess home is . . . earth . . . but I'm not an earth elf like Farran."

"Do you live underwater? Or in the sky?" Aira had a lot of questions. She pulled out a small notebook to record Emily's answers. "Oh, do you have dragons?"

"We definitely do not have dragons! Uh, do you?" When Aira nodded absently, Emily, shocked, started to look around for one. Then

Azari announced, "Enough questions. Let's get going!"

It seemed to Emily that Azari was always in a hurry.

Farran was the opposite. He carefully hefted his sack over his shoulder. "Okay. I think I have everything I need to figure out this portal." He started walking toward the forest, but after a few steps realized Aira and Azari weren't following. "Come on," Farran said. "This way!"

"Yeah, but no," Azari told him. "Aira and I agree. We are going to look for another way to get Emily home."

"Huh?" Farran asked. "But it's a tree, and I know trees. As long as we go in with a plan, this should be as easy as—"

"I already tried reopening the portal. It didn't work," Azari told him. "We're moving on."

"Wait a second—" Farran argued. "You're fire. I'm earth. There's a difference. I can do magic you can't." He quickly added, "And you can do magic that I can't."

"Sorry, Farran," Aira cut in. "I think Azari is right. We have to find another way to send Emily home."

Farran was insulted. "Another way? There is no other way! What we need is a big bag of tools and a supersmart earth elf who knows how to use them!"

Azari snorted. "And where would we find this supersmart earth elf?"

Farran pointed to himself. "Isn't it obvious?"

Aira laughed then said, "Farran, this might

sound nutty, but I actually know an old story about a portal that might be related. It's in a castle. It's crazy hard to get to, and there are something like four keys to open it."

"That's ridiculous. Sounds like a myth to me, which means it's not true," Farran said.

Emily hadn't been sure if she should try to step into the elves' discussion, but now she was really curious. She loved stories.

"Can you tell me the whole story?" she asked. "I've never heard it."

"Sure!" Aira agreed. "It's the legend of the five sisters. Four of them were elves of different elements."

"Like us?" Azari asked. "Earth, fire, and wind!"

"Exactly!" Aira said. "And water, of course. But the fifth sister had no magic. After a long search, she found a place where there were others like her, and decided to live there instead. She left Elvendale through a portal."

At the word *portal*, Emily's heart raced. Could the story be about the same magical passage she'd come through?

"Why would anyone want to live in a world without magic? How boring!" Azari gasped.

"Uh . . . I do," Emily said, pointing to herself. "It's not that bad."

"Oh, right," Azari said. "Um. There are probably some interesting things in your world, too. Sorry!"

The legend was exciting to Emily. Maybe it could even help her get home! "What else do you know about the portal in the story?" Emily asked Aira.

Aira thought for a moment. "I remember

that the elves actually built two portals," she said at last. "One to enter and one to leave. The one to leave Elvendale was in the castle."

"I bet the one to enter was in a tree!" Emily bounced up on her toes. "If it was, that would explain why I couldn't return home through it."

"But it's a myth!" Farran repeated. No one paid him any attention.

Aira said, "To protect the portal, the elf sisters made magic keys. It took all four of their keys to open the portal from this side."

"Can we find those keys?" Azari asked, and Farran rolled his eyes.

"I wish I knew how," Aira said. "The story goes that the fifth sister became mortal and began to grow older in her new world. Eventually, she stopped visiting. Without her, the sisters who lived here grew apart." She gave a long sigh. "The keys were lost. It's even possible that the castle disappeared."

"If there was ever a castle at all," Farran said. "Look, using a legend as our guide is not very practical. Instead of looking for mythical keys to an imaginary castle with a pretend portal, we need to get back to the portal that we know actually existed and send Emily back through there."

"Forget it, Farran," Azari told him. "We can't go backward. We've gotta go forward!"

"Yes! Forward to the forest!" Farran announced.

"That portal is closed. We need to find the second one," Aira put in. "Could there be a map to the castle?"

"A map?" Azari echoed, her eyes lighting up.

"We don't need a map! There's no castle!" Farran countered.

"Don't be such a wet blanket of moss! We're going on an adventure!" Azari exclaimed. "And we are gonna find those keys."

Farran moaned and rolled his eyes.

Emily piped up. "We have to do something, or I may never get home!" She'd promised her parents she was only going on a short walk. She needed to get back before dark!

Farran started heading toward the forest again.

"Give it up, Farran!" Azari called after him.

Aira told Emily, "Come on. We are going to visit Naida. If a map exists, she'll know about it."

Though Emily didn't know who Naida was, she decided to go with the girls. But she also didn't want to leave Farran behind. And what if he was right about the tree? As they walked away from the forest, Emily was filled with nerves. She kept glancing back over her shoulder, watching as Farran got farther away.

Azari was far ahead, but Aira walked next to Emily. "He'll catch up. He always does," the wind elf whispered. "I bet he'll say something about how much we'll need him."

They were about to cross a little bridge over a stream when Emily heard Farran's voice coming over the meadow.

"Oh, fine," he called, his tool bag clanking. "I'll come. You're going to need me."

"Told you." Aira winked.

Emily couldn't help but smile.

Chapter 4

The Map

Naida was a water elf. She lived in a vast system of caves full of hidden waterfalls and rivers, opening up to a beautiful ocean view. Elvendale was full of surprises—Emily had not stopped being amazed.

When they entered Naida's caves, Emily completely understood why they'd come. There were smaller caves carved out in Naida's walls that were full of scrolls. Naida was standing near a whirling tidal pool in a flowing dress of many different shades of blue.

Azari marched over. "Naida, we need your wisdom! What do you know about the legend of the sisters and the four keys?"

"Not much," Naida admitted. She was distracted by a chirping noise that Emily realized was coming from a dolphin in the water. "What?" Pause. Then, "Oh, thanks, Delphia," Naida said to the dolphin. Then she explained, "My place is a mess." She ran a hand through her long blue hair. "Delphia is helping me clean up."

Naida could talk to dolphins! It was clear they understood each other, and were close friends. Emily wished she could talk to animals!

"Naida?" Azari interrupted whatever she was saying to Delphia. "About the five sisters?"

"Oh. Right." Naida swept her hair back over her shoulder and said, "Well, I don't know much, but I can tell you—hey! Wait a minute!" She turned her head to Emily. "Do I know you?"

Emily laughed. She loved how Naida's brain spun at a million miles an hour.

"Hi, I'm Emily," she said, and explained how she got there.

"I like your ears," Naida whispered as Azari joined in with her own explanation. "So we need a map of Elvendale! An old one," Azari finished.

"I've got tons of maps," Naida said, waving an arm around the caves.

"If you'd just let me invent something to help, your collection would be a lot more organized," Aira moaned. "Delphia wouldn't have to work so hard."

"Thanks, but I'm okay," Naida said. "Delphia and I have things under control—most of the time." Everyone laughed.

Naida walked to the ocean's edge and talked softly to Delphia. The dolphin dove deep and disappeared from view.

"She'll be right back," Naida told them. "Delphia says she knows what you need."

Suddenly, Delphia reappeared, flipping high in the air, bumping her nose against a shelf near the top of the room. When she returned to Naida, she presented a tightly wound scroll.

"Thanks!" Naida said.

She carefully spread the parchment on the table. It was an old map labeled "Elvendale."

"Good work, Delphia," Naida called to her friend.

The map was a large drawing on faded

yellow parchment. The center of the land was marked with mountains and hills and pathways connecting cities with crazy names like Highland of Helyan and Enki Island. "Look, there's a castle!" Emily said, pointing. The map seemed to shimmer around the image of a fortress in the mountains.

"Where?" Farran squeezed between the girls. "Let me see."

They all pored over the document, and Naida lifted it up to look more closely. All of a sudden the image began to move and shift, swirling and glittering!

"Magic," Naida said calmly, as if this always happened.

As they watched, the swirling slowed, and the mountains and lakes and forests settled back in place.

Naida studied it closely, "Hang on. There's something else here." The map was shimmering in one area. "Check it out! There's a picture of a key here," Naida said, then muttered, "Only one, though. Shouldn't there be four? Hmm."

Aira took the map from Naida. "I want to see! Wait, it's all moving around. I think I see . . . Look, there's a different key now!"

She turned the map to Naida. "When you held the map, a key appeared by the ocean. Now this one is floating above the tallest mountain."

Azari grabbed the map from Aira. It shimmered in her hands as well. "And now there's a different key! It's near the volcano."

She held out the map to Farran. "Let's see what happens when you try!"

In Farran's hands, the map shimmered again,

and another key appeared. This time it was at a spot called Sparkle Rock.

"Four keys and a castle, just like the legend," Emily breathed. "It must be true." She felt a huge sense of excitement bubbling inside her. This magic was real!

Azari punched Farran in the arm. "Not a fairy tale anymore, is it?"

Farran shrugged. "I always believed," he said, tapping his heart. "I was just kidding around before . . ."

Azari snorted at him. "Well, should we go find the keys?"

"How long do you think it will take?" Emily asked. "My parents are probably already really worried that they can't find me."

"I don't know," Azari said. "All the more reason to hurry! Who even knows if this magic map will show us where they are again, so we'd better start while we remember."

Suddenly, Emily realized that she was asking a lot of these elves. "Maybe I should go find them on my own," she suggested. It would be hard, but it was her problem. She didn't even have anything to give the elves in return for helping her. "I mean, we just met, and I'm sure you have other things you need to be doing."

"You're being silly," Azari said. "We love adventure!" She quickly added, "Well, except for Farran."

"Yes . . . but I like returning lost things," Farran told her. "And you are lost."

"I like helping," Aira reminded her. "And I'd love to see that castle!"

"One other thing," Naida said. She passed the map to Emily. In her hands, the map showed the ocean and the mountains and the island . . . but no keys. "Just like I thought," Naida said. "You need us to find the keys!"

Just as Emily was going to respond, the map began swirling again. No keys appeared— instead, there was a fancy script message in a language Emily didn't know. Azari translated: *"Greetings, Four Elements and Girl from Another World. You will need each other to claim the legacy of the sisters."*

Emily could hardly breathe. The map knew about *her*, the girl from another world. How was that possible?!

"See?!" Azari said. "We all have to go! The map told us to stick together. So. Naida's key is the closest, somewhere in the sea. Let's go there first!" She handed Naida the map and the girls all started walking toward a boat docked at the far end of the cave.

Farran had put his hand over his heart like he was reciting a pledge. "Now, more than ever, we must unite to help Emily on her journey," he proclaimed. "Even if it means leaving our homes, and—hey! Where did everybody go?"

As Emily glanced back at Farran, he was already running to catch up.

Chapter 5

Onto the Sea

The sun warmed Emily's face as she and the others rested on the boat's deck, sailing slowly toward the first key.

Too slowly, Emily thought. Not that she wanted to go at Azari's rocket speed, but this wasn't even Farran's snail pace. They seemed to be stopped.

"Um . . . Are we moving?" Emily asked the elves.

Azari had her eyes closed. "We're going so fast you can't feel it, right Naida?"

"Actually . . . we've stopped." Naida admitted, looking over the edge..

"Looks like we ran out of wind," Farran remarked.

Aira was on it. "Right. I'll make a windmill. Or a supersized sail. Maybe some wings . . ." Emily could practically see her mind spinning.

"Um, Aira, can't you control the wind?" Emily asked. "Could you just make it *windy*?"

Azari giggled. "Em's right." She paused and looked at Emily, "Can I call you Em?"

"Sure." Emily smiled. "My grandmother used to call me that sometimes."

Azari grinned.

Farran said, "I'll re-rig the sails, then Aira can give us a breeze to get us going!"

"Maybe you can help, since you're full of hot air!" Azari said, chuckling. Farran rolled his eyes.

"Here we go!" Aira raised her arms, focused, and started creating wind. While she worked, Aira sang quietly—which didn't hide that she was tone-deaf! Emily would have laughed, but if singing helped Aira make wind, they'd all learn to enjoy it.

As the boat picked up speed, Emily went to Naida, who had one hand on the steering wheel and the other on the map. An image of Naida's key had thankfully returned, glittering directly over water.

Finally, Naida announced, "This should be the place!" She dropped anchor.

Azari looked around. "All I see is a bunch of ocean."

Naida was studying the map again when a misty fog covered most of the image. When it cleared, a new message had appeared. "Looks like we have a clue to help us get the key!" Naida exclaimed. *"What you seek rests next to the mermaid's tears."*

All the elves looked thoughtful. "Do you guys understand it?" Emily asked. Everyone shook their heads.

Mermaids—there were so many magical creatures to know about! It made Emily want to stay and explore more of Elvendale, but she really did need to get home. She had her regular life to get back to. And at Grandmother's house, it would be dark soon—her parents would be very upset that she hadn't returned. She wished there was a way to tell them she was safe and trying to get home.

"Mermaid's tears . . ." Emily repeated the clue over to herself. There was a memory nagging at the back of her mind. "I—" she started, then stopped. It was frustrating not being able to remember something so important. "Wait . . . Mermaid's tear!" Emily suddenly jumped up and rushed to Naida. "I have an idea that might be a hint!"

"What?!" all the elves shouted at once.

Emily said, "Well, when my grandfather Richard proposed to marry Grandmother, instead of a traditional engagement diamond, he gave her a small rose-colored pearl. Grandmother loved it—she always said the pearl glittered in the moonlight like a mermaid's tear." Emily had also once asked Grandmother how she knew what a mermaid's tear looked like, but she had just smiled mysteriously.

"That's so romantic," Aira said breathily. "True love."

"Uck," Farran rolled his eyes. "I prefer stories with more excitement—you know, like if your grandfather saved your grandmother from the jaws of a scary sea monster!"

Emily laughed. "I don't think that ever happened."

"Too bad," Farran said with a grumble.

"Anyway, could mermaid's tears have something to do with pearls?" Emily asked.

"Of course! Yes!" Naida replied. "Emily, that's it—thank you!" She leaned over the side of the boat, and so did everyone else. Looking down into the clear blue water, they all saw the bottom at once. "Oysters!"

"We are at Oyster Cove!" Naida raised her arms and began using her water power to split the sea and raise a shell to the surface. Her hair glistened with droplets of water, and a fine mist swirled around her. Soon she held a large oyster, and pried open the rough shell. "No key."

"Did you really think it was going to be inside the first one you checked?" Farran asked.

Naida shrugged. "I was hoping . . ."

"Well, that one doesn't have the key, and now he looks angry," Farran said. "I'm not sure we should be prying open their shells like this. Oysters have lives, too, you know . . ."

Aira joined in. "Plus, there must be a million oysters down there. We will never find the right one if we're just picking randomly!"

Emily's heart sank. "Could we skip to another key?" she suggested. "Farran's showed up not far from here, right?"

Naida handed the map to Farran, but it didn't swirl, and the key image stayed in place. No matter which elf held it, the map didn't budge.

Emily wished she had another idea. They had to keep moving! If they failed, she'd never get home!

"Ouch!" Naida shouted as the oyster she held snapped its shell closed on her finger. She shook it off, tossing it back into the ocean.

Aira had been thinking. "Naida, can you tell us everything you know about oysters, pearls, and mermaids?"

They all turned to the water elf. She was rubbing the red tip of her finger where the oyster had clamped down. "Oysters create pearls from grains of sand that get into their shells," Naida said. "The sand is annoying, so they make a milky smooth layer to put over it again and again until—"

"Wait," Emily interrupted. "If a tiny grain of sand is annoying to an oyster, imagine what a large key might feel like! A key is probably too big to coat with a smooth essence. It must really hurt. I feel bad for the poor oyster."

"You have such a soft, loving heart, Emily," Aira said, smiling. "It's nice."

"And helpful," Naida said. "I'll be right back."

Naida again raised her hands over the water, this time spinning it into a whirling vortex with a water staircase in the middle. Naida climbed out onto the steps, glowing with a blue light as she descended into water. At the bottom, she reached out to the oysters as if speaking to them. Some opened their shells; others rolled away.

Suddenly, the water churned and the sea turned a murky brown color, filled with bubbles and rocking wild waves. They couldn't see Naida anymore.

"Oh no!" Emily exclaimed as the boat swished from side to side in the rough waves. "It looks like Naida's in trouble!"

Aira called up wind to push back the water, but they couldn't see Naida.

"We shouldn't have come," Farran moaned.

Just then, the water cleared, the staircase reappeared, and Naida stepped onto the boat. In her hand, she held a turquoise-colored key that sparkled in the sunlight.

They all rushed over to her.

"What happened?" Azari asked.

"We were worried!" Emily said.

"That oyster sure was angry," Naida told them. "Just like Emily said, I had to find the unhappiest one. The one who was in the most pain." She raised the key. "I did, and now he feels better!"

"I'm glad we could help him," Emily said.

"And he helped us!" Naida added, staring at the glittering key.

"We got the first key! Woo!" Azari exclaimed.

The group's excitement was back, and they congratulated each other with high fives.

"It's getting dark," Farran said. "Let's sleep on the boat and look for the next key in the morning."

Everyone agreed. Emily was impatient to keep going, but she was also exhausted from the day's adventure. Finding the other keys would be easier after a rest.

They all settled in for the night, and Emily let the slow rock of the waves soothe her. The stars were twinkling in the sky above. Were those the same stars her parents could see at home?

Chapter 6

Sparkle Rock

Emily thought she would fall right to sleep, but worry and doubt were bubbling back up, keeping her awake. Perhaps she should have pushed the group to keep going overnight. She'd been gone for a long time. Had her parents called the police by now? Were they searching for her?

Emily missed them, and she missed home. She let out a long, heavy sigh.

"Are you still up?" Azari asked.

It turned out the others were having a hard time falling asleep as well.

"We need a bedtime story," Naida suggested. "I have about a thousand different ones in my head. Which one do you want to hear?"

"Or I could sing a song," Aira suggested.

"No!" they all shouted together.

Emily said, "When I was young, I liked to go to sleep with a song my grandmother sang to me. Would you like to hear it?"

"Yes!" Aira said. "I'd love to hear more about your grandmother."

"The song is about never being alone, and it always made me feel safe," Emily told them. She began to sing:

"Earth moves the air,
And the wind feeds the fire.

Magic is here,
If you dare to believe!
Sail out to sea
On an ocean of mystery,
And bring your heart
To the ones that you meet."

Emily loved singing, and was in the school choir. Grandmother had never missed a performance, and always clapped the loudest. School songs were fun, but Grandmother's song was her favorite.

Emily hummed the song once more to herself with her eyes closed, holding her blue medallion. She started to feel calmer—and the next thing she knew, it was morning.

Farran was standing above her shouting, "Wake up!" He was acting like Azari, waving the map around. "It's glowing! Let's move it!"

They docked the boat at Sparkle Rock and walked deep into the forest, toward where the key seemed to be. As they got closer, a mist rose off the map again, and new text appeared. Farran read the clue aloud. *"The pockets of the earth are never empty, yet they can be hard to dig into."*

Farran was irritated. "That's just nonsense. Naida's clue was so easy. Why is mine so hard?"

"Mine wasn't easy," Naida said. "Emily just figured it out." All the elves looked at her.

Azari asked, "What do you think it means?"

Emily frowned. "I'm not sure. Could it have to do with money? Money can fill your pocket."

"Money?" Azari asked. "What's that?"

"We use it to pay for stuff," Emily said. "Never mind."

"Can you think of anything else?" Naida asked.

Emily thought more. "What if 'pockets of earth' are holes in the ground, like animal burrows? When Grandmother and I walked in her garden, she always pointed them out to me."

"Yes!" Farran said. "And the pockets are never empty, because there are always living things under the ground, even if the animal isn't home."

"So we have to find the right animal burrow!" Emily exclaimed.

"But what does 'they can be hard to dig into' mean?" Naida asked.

"I think that finding the key is going to be hard," Aira said. "It's a warning."

"Uh-oh." Farran sighed.

"Let's start exploring!" Azari cried.

Emily proudly showed them how Grandmother taught her to spot the "pockets" where the animals made their homes.

Farran took over, using his earth senses to lead them up a hill and down another, until he raised his arms and shouted, "Stop! This is the place! I can feel it!"

Before them was an enormous stone. It was gray streaked with black, and there was a little cave opening near the ground. A squirrel was running back and forth territorially in front of it.

"If only we could speak squirrel . . ." Emily said, looking at the furry creature.

"I've got this one," Farran said, approaching the rock. "Hello, squirrel, I'm—" He paused when the squirrel said something back in a chattery squeak. "Oh, excuse me," Farran said.

"Hello, Miss Spry. I'm Farran, earth elf. We request your assistance—"

Again the squirrel interrupted him, but this time not with chatter. She bared her teeth and waved her little paws, trying to scare the group away.

"This fur-ball thinks it can scare us?" Azari snorted.

Farran said, "Miss Spry, if we could just—" He gasped at whatever she said. "There's no need for that kind of language!"

"I think she's protecting something," Emily said.

"Farran, ask fur-face about her storage facility," Azari said.

Miss Spry growled and started launching nuts at Farran's head with a tiny twig catapult.

He ducked, saying, "Does she look like she wants to talk?!" Without warning, Miss Spry leapt up onto Farran's head and grabbed onto his hair. *"Ahhhhhh!"* he shouted. "Get off me!"

Naida began using her magic to draw water from a nearby stream. She tossed it on Miss Spry, who finally let go, scampering back down in front of the rock. Farran was dripping wet.

"You're welcome," Naida said with a smile.

Farran shook himself off, then said, "Let's try something else." Kneeling to the ground, he closed his eyes, put his hands on the soil, and moved them in a slow pattern. A green glow surrounded him, and plants began sprouting and twirling around him. Emily was entranced. Finally, he stood. "The key is back in that cave, but there are too many rocks in the way for me to get to it right now."

"Just like your head." Azari laughed. "Full of rocks!"

"That must be the *'hard to dig into'* part of the clue," Emily realized.

Farran nodded. "Okay. I'm going to get the key out, but it's going to get messy, dangerous, and a bit—"

"Just do it!" Azari shouted.

"I am!" he shouted back.

Emily laughed at the two of them, bickering like brother and sister. Aira was far more encouraging. "Go on," she said. "We know you can do this."

The air became electric as Farran directed his magic toward the trees, as if he were conducting an earth symphony. The regular noises

64

of the forest stopped. Roots appeared, slithering like snakes over the forest floor toward the cave.

Suddenly, Farran stood tall, and shouted, "RUN!"

With a deep groan and a crash, the huge stone in front of them cracked, and a mighty rockslide began. Farran had warned them just in time. With a swooping leap, he grabbed Miss Spry, too.

When the dust settled, they could see where the cave had been.

"Way to go, Farran!" Emily cried happily. "Look!"

Nestled on the ground between nuts and sparkling gemstones was a shining green key.

Farran reached out for it, but Miss Spry bounded forward, blocking his way.

"Come on," he told her. "We're not the enemy here. We just gave you access to all these blocked acorns—and gems! Just let us have that key."

After a moment's consideration, Miss Spry moved aside.

Farran shook her little paw, then grabbed the key and waved it above his head. "I did it!" he said, and they all cheered. "All right," Farran said, handing Azari the map. "Your turn. Good luck."

Chapter 7

The Lava Field

The sun was high as they boarded Naida's boat to head back to the mainland. With Aira blowing the sails and Farran at the mast, they soon reached the shore. Emily was confident that with Azari in the lead, they'd have the third key in no time—which was good, because the passage of time was making her more and more nervous about what was happening back at home. Were her parents frantic? Were the police searching the neighborhood? Emily shivered at that last thought. But she was doing her best to get back. She turned her attention to Azari, hoping the map would reveal another clue.

They were soon walking through a forest toward the Lava Field. Emily was surprised that it felt so different from the forest at Sparkle Rock. There it was cooler, and very shady. Here, the air felt warm, and there was a slight smoky smell. In the distance, she could see a small mountain with a low black cloud covering the peak. Was that a volcano?!

"Are we going there?" Emily asked. All she knew about volcanoes was that they were very dangerous!

"Of course," Azari told her, looking down at the glowing map. "We're in the lava lands now, Em, and I'm all aglow!"

Emily chuckled. Azari's jokes were bad, but they lightened her mood.

Soon, a new clue appeared on the map, and Azari read it out loud. *"A curtain of gold falls between you and what you need."* She frowned. "What could that mean?!"

"A curtain might be like on a stage," Farran said, trying to help.

"I'm an expert in falling," Naida said with a small smile. "That's what happens when you try to think and walk at the same time."

Azari sighed. "Let's just stick to getting closer to the key," she said. "We can solve the clue later. This way."

As they approached the volcano, Emily had to admit that it was pretty majestic. A puff of smoke came from the top, and lava stretched down the side, glowing bright red and yellow mixed with black. As it reached the bottom, it oozed over rough dark rocks into a glittering sunset-colored lava pool.

Emily walked faster to keep up with Azari as they veered down a narrow path.

"That pool at the bottom looks so much like water!" Naida remarked.

Azari explained, "The hottest lava is the brightest color. As it cools, the lava turns from that brilliant orange to a shimmering red, then to dark red, then brown, and finally black when it's solid." She looked around, then exclaimed, "Hey, we're near the bakery! Let's go. But we have to walk carefully through here. Follow me, and try to step only where I step."

They lined up and stayed close together. The lava smelled bad, like burned tires, but soon there was also a waft of something delicious nearby. It reminded Emily of the scrumptious scent of Grandmother's kitchen when she was making her famous cookies!

Just past the next rocky outcrop, Emily was amazed to see why: There was a bakery right by the lava pool! It was a small shack with open windows. Each window ledge was filled with steaming treats.

A fox sat outside the bakery. Its red, bushy tail waved as if greeting the visitors.

Azari called out, "Hey, Flamy, how's it going?" She turned toward Emily. "He's a fire fox."

A moment later, a boy burst out of the bakery. His red clothing looked very similar to Azari's dress, and in his hands was a tray piled with cookies, cinnamon buns, bagels, and bread slices.

"Johnny!" Azari rushed to hug him.

"Hey, Azari!" he said. "Want some fresh baked goods? I recommend the cinnamon buns!"

Aira's hand was almost to the tray when Azari blocked the way.

"Priorities, Johnny Baker," Azari told him. "We have to find a key before we can eat!"

But Azari was out-voted, and the elves and Emily swarmed Johnny and his tray.

While Naida enjoyed a thick piece of sweet bread, Emily ate several cookies. "Just like my grandmother's," Emily said, licking her lips. "Thanks."

Azari gave in and had a few treats, too. They all munched happily.

Johnny soon offered Emily another cookie, but she declined. "I can't eat another bite. I'm so full!"

So he wrapped some cookies up for her, saying, "Here's some for later!"

Emily took them and thanked him.

Azari looked at the map again. "I know the third key's right around here," she said. "But this clue is a mystery. *'A curtain of gold falls between you and what you need.'* Pff! I don't see any curtains here!"

"I live here, and I don't know what that means," Johnny said. "I don't even have curtains in my house because they catch fire so easily!"

Azari heaved a big sigh.

"Is there anything gold in the bakery?" Emily asked.

"You mean, other than my luscious gold hair?" Johnny said, winking. "I'm not sure, but I can show you around." The elves all followed him into the kitchen, and he explained how the volcano lava created heat for the ovens. When he showed them a panel of buttons and switches, Aira's eyes lit up.

"I'd like a closer look at the valve casings and the knobs," Aira said, rubbing her chin. "I might even have some ideas for how to improve your cooking system . . ."

"You're welcome to visit any time!" Johnny said as Azari dragged Aira away from the panel. Flamy the fox ran by, and Johnny said, "Oh, better check the oven! He tells me when the cakes are done."

"Like a timer?" Emily said. She explained how Grandmother used a small alarm clock to tell her when her treats were ready.

"Exactly," Johnny said. "Flamy's a very talented fire fox!"

"Flamy, have you seen the key?" Azari asked. He howled at her. Azari frowned. "Nope."

They all went back outside. Emily was starting to get anxious again. They had to find that key!

"What could be a curtain of gold?" she asked. "My necklace chain is silver, so that's not it." Grandmother's medallion hung cool around her neck.

Farran said, "Johnny's bread is gold-colored."

"Sunsets can be gold," Aira said dreamily. "Though we'd have to wait around all day for that. Or if we waited all summer, autumn leaves are gold, too."

Suddenly, Emily had a thought. "Something gold IS falling!"

"What? Where?!" Johnny's head spun as he looked all around.

"Lava!" Emily pointed toward the lava pool and the way the lava flowed down into it over the rocks, like a small waterfall.

"That's not really falling, it's more just slowly flowing . . ." Farran said. But Azari was going over to it with her arms outstretched, glowing red, her hair sparking.

"Azari's all fired up!" Johnny joked.

"You were right again, Em! This is the place!" Azari exclaimed.

Johnny and Farran looked at her skeptically.

"The key is behind the lava." Azari turned to Johnny and asked, "Is there a path that goes behind the lavafall?"

"No," Johnny said. "Even with fire powers, you can't get there."

Everyone was silent for a moment, and Azari took a different approach to the lava flow, stepping on cool black stones within the little lava lake. With a flick of her wrist, she magically moved the lava curtain to the side, revealing the key! But when she went to reach for it with her other hand, the curtain closed again.

"I can't keep the lava curtain open and grab the key at the same time!" She turned back to look at the others. "What do we do?"

"There's not room for another person to even get close," Aira said.

Emily's mind was racing. They were so close to getting this key!

"Aira!" Farran exclaimed. "Build a heat-resistant, fireproof key-grabber!"

Aira looked around. "Hmm. I could use parts from Johnny's kitchen and add some sticks and a long vine. If we could put together some sort of engine, I could start to . . ." Her words died away as she realized how impossible that all would be. "I wish," she ended. "But I can't."

Emily noticed that Flamy had come out of bakery again, and looked curious.

"Can we get the fox to help?" Emily suggested.

"Great idea!" Azari said. She quickly explained the situation to Flamy, and he nodded. "You can do it, boy!" she said.

She raised her arms with fresh determination, splitting the lava curtain into two hot golden halves. Flamy leapt right through the center.

The fire fox looked like a flame himself! Fear seized Emily—what if she had just put the fox in danger?! But no one else seemed to be worried.

"Yes!" Azari cheered. "Thatta boy! Go on, Flamy!"

Flamy leapt back out between the molten flow and dropped a red key at Azari's feet.

"Unbelievable!" Emily cried.

Azari hugged the fox. Emily ran forward to hug him, too, but Azari stopped her. "Em, no! He still needs to cool down."

"Right," she said, backing up. "Of course." She gave him a little wave instead. "Thanks, Flamy. You're the best."

"Yes!" Naida gave a clumsy high five to everyone in reach. "We have three of the four keys now! This is brilliant!"

"Just one more," Azari said, snatching up the key. "Then, hopefully, off to the castle." She thrust the map to Aira. "Don't let us down!"

Chapter 8

Up in the Air

Locating the final key was proving to be more difficult than they first thought. The map had showed it on top of a mountain, which Emily and the elves had been climbing for hours. But after they got partway up, the image of the key started moving! It had been moving around on the map ever since, but kept coming back to the mountain they were on.

They stopped for a break. Everyone was breathing heavily.

"The clue hasn't even appeared yet!" Emily complained. Her toes hurt. She wished she'd worn boots into Grandmother's garden instead of her cute, but flimsy, sneakers.

"Why won't the key stay still?" Aira asked, frustrated.

"We'll never catch it!" Naida moaned. Azari and Farran were up ahead, scouting the area.

Emily and Aira studied the map some more. The key went from the highest mountain peak to a valley to a steep cliff. "I bet the key is in the sky!" Aira realized. She held her arms up, concentrating, and starting to give off a light purple glow. But then she stopped. "I can't bring it any closer with my magic. Hey, maybe I could build us a net!"

"I could call over some vines to help make it," Farran said. "But I don't know if a net can move fast enough to catch that thing."

"This mountain is too high," Azari said. This was the first time that Emily had heard her sounding so discouraged.

"Maybe we should turn back," Naida said.

"But we need that key," Azari replied with a heavy groan.

"We just might not be able to get it," Aira countered.

"Emily could live in the water caves with me," Naida suggested.

That comment made Emily's heart start to pound heavily. Elvendale was beautiful and magical, but it wasn't her home! She needed to find a way back. And now the group was arguing about whether or not they should even still try to find the fourth key!

Emily stepped away, feeling overwhelmed by the possibility of failure. She sat with her head on her knees, breathing deeply, trying not to cry.

Soon she felt a hand on her shoulder. It was Naida, who asked, "Are you okay?"

Emily shook her head and let it all out in a burst. "I'm sorry," she said with a sniff. "I just feel homesick. It seems like we're so close, but it also seems so impossible. Even if we do figure out how to get the key, we still don't know if we can find the portal! And if we do find the portal, can we can open it?" She sniffed one more time. "I know you meant well when you said I could stay with you, but I want to go home. I'm starting to be afraid I may never see my family again."

By this time, everyone else had stopped bickering and moved closer to Emily. "I'm so sorry, Emily," Azari said.

"I know!" Aira announced. "To cheer us all up, I could sing!"

"No!" everyone else exclaimed, their voices echoing off the mountain.

Azari quickly followed with, "We mean, uh, no thanks. But maybe Emily could sing her grandmother's song again. It was so nice."

Emily agreed, thinking that the song would at least help take her mind off her heartache. She felt so much love from her grandmother whenever she sang the song. Maybe it would give them added strength to track down that last key!

She felt a tingle inside as she started to hum at first, then sang the words:

"Earth moves the air,
And the wind feeds the fire.
Magic is here
If you dare to believe . . ."

Suddenly, the trees began to sway and a heavy breeze blew dirt around them. Emily looked up and saw two winged horses flying their way!

"Wow. Pegasi!" Naida exclaimed. "I don't know if you have any of those in your world, Emily, but seeing even one pegasus is rare in Elvendale."

Emily couldn't tear her eyes away from the amazing creatures. The winged horses had snow-white, unblemished coats. They soared through the air, gentle and graceful, as if on clouds. She felt like they must have come for a reason.

"Beautiful!" Emily gasped. "Aira, can you talk to them, since they fly?"

"It can't hurt to ask them to help us," Naida encouraged Aira.

Aira looked thoughtful. "I've only tweeted birds before. You would not believe how much they gossip! But pegasi do have wings . . ."

She raised her arms toward the horses, sending magic their way. Emily felt a new surge of hope—which changed to panic as the pegasi sped down toward them at lightning speed!

"Are they going to stop in time?" Emily shouted.

They did, landing lightly near Aira. She approached them slowly, bowing respectfully as she went. Soon Aira was whispering softly to them. Emily looked on in awe.

Aira turned to the others, face shining. "Their names are Starshine and Rufus—and they want to help!"

As everyone gathered around the pegasi, Aira said to Emily, "It was your song."

"What?" Emily didn't understand. "Grandmother's song?"

"Actually, I don't think I am explaining this right," Aira said. "It wasn't the actual tune. Starshine told me they'd been called here by a feeling. It was like a magnet that pulled them to us. I think it was *you*."

"Wow!" Emily said. That wasn't what she had been expecting.

Aira smiled. "Just thought you should know." She spoke with the winged horses again, then announced, "Two pegasi can't carry four elves and a girl up a mountain."

"Darn it!" Azari exclaimed. "Should we split up?"

Emily felt like there must be a way for them to stick together. She looked around, really paying attention to their surroundings for the first time in a while—she'd been too wrapped up in her homesickness to notice much before. There was a windmill nearby!

She called to the others, "Could two pegasi pull us all in some sort of cart?"

Farran turned in the direction Emily was looking. "Oh! We can use wood from that windmill," he said.

"Yes! We'll make a sleigh!" Aira exclaimed, and started shouting instructions to everyone. They all got to work.

Farran's tools came in handy, though the sleigh they built still ended up a little rickety.

"Do you think it'll fly?" Emily asked Farran.

"It might, but it won't be safe," he replied, looking skeptical.

Azari, usually so brave, was starting to turn the same shade of green as Farran's clothing the longer she looked at the sleigh. "This might be a bad idea," Azari said as Aira connected the sleigh to the pegasi.

They all climbed on board, and the horses started flapping their wings. As Aira began using her wind magic, the sleigh rose from the ground. Emily felt a thrill run through her.

Farran was clearly trying to be supportive, and let out a weak, "Wahoo!" but then closed his eyes and clenched his seat.

"It's still not too late to change our minds!" Azari muttered, grabbing Emily for support.

Emily was surprised that she didn't feel scared. She trusted Aira's magic, and knowing that there was something about *her* that had brought the pegasi to them gave her strength.

"Starshine and Rufus, give us wings!" Aira shouted as she called forth a strong gust of wind.

They lifted off. Emily tingled with nerves and excitement.

"This is *amaaaaaaazing*!" she shrieked. In Elvendale, the magical surprises never seemed to end!

Naida laughed as the wind whipped her hair. She was loving it as much as Emily. "I'm always in water," she said. "But flying is wonderful!"

"Now where is that key?" Aira asked. "It must be somewhere near here." She scanned the sky.

"Find it fast so we can slow down!" Azari begged.

Naida said, "Look at the map—it's still showing the key moving all over the place."

Finally, the clue appeared. Aira read the golden letters. *"The key is a mouthful . . ."*

"Is that it? That doesn't make sense," Farran said. "But *'mouthful'* reminds me that I'm kind of hungry."

"You are not!" Azari told him. "We are in a scary situation. It's not the time for snacks!"

"Danger makes me hungry!" He rubbed his tummy.

"I have some of Johnny's cookies," Emily said, pulling them out.

Farran reached for one, then immediately dropped it into the sky. *"Draaaaagoooon!"*

"What did he say?" Emily asked Naida,

watching the cookie fall and fall toward the earth until it disappeared from sight.

Naida touched Emily's arm, then pointed up. Above them on a mountain ledge sat a dragon. A real dragon! Emily was in shock.

The dragon took off, circling once around them, then landing back on his perch.

Emily was looking at the map in Aira's hands.

"Did you see that?" she asked the elves.

"No!" Farran said. "My eyes are closed."

"Mine, too," Azari admitted.

"When the dragon circled us, so did the key on the map." Emily considered the clue. *"Mouthful.* Oh no!"

"You know where the key is?" Aira asked.

"I think the fourth key is in the dragon's mouth! That's the answer to the riddle," Emily said. The elves all gasped, but Emily was lost in thought, remembering the snapdragons in the garden, the flowers that looked like tiny little dragon mouths. What had Grandmother said about them? *"Dragons get mean when they are hungry, so be sure to feed them treats and keep their tummies full. I hear they like cookies."* Cookies!

"Aira?" Emily asked, "Can you make cookies fly?"

A few moments later, Aira gently tossed a cookie up to the dragon, keeping it afloat longer than would've been possible without magic. The dragon spotted it and leapt after it eagerly. He dove for it, but missed. Aira tossed another and another, but each time the dragon missed the cookie.

"C'mon! Save the chocolate chip ones," Farran said, rubbing his belly.

"Sorry," Emily said, handing Aira the final cookie. "This is the last one!"

The dragon was ready—and when he opened his mouth to snatch it up, something shiny fell out.

"There it is!" Emily pointed at the glittering speck falling fast toward the earth below. "The key!"

"We'll never find it if it hits the ground," Azari yelled at Aira. "Do something!"

"On it!" Aira steered the pegasi downward. The sleigh dove straight toward the ground.

Azari screamed. Farran's mouth was wide open in terror, but no sound came out.

Emily felt dizzy as the sleigh jolted and spiraled toward the sharp rocks below.

"Where's Aira?" Naida said suddenly.

Emily snapped her head to look. Aira wasn't at the reins!

"Whaddya mean, where's Aira?!" Azari shrieked.

Farran found his voice. "What is *haaapppennnninnnngg*?!"

A loud whistle brought Emily's attention to the side of the sleigh. She leaned over, and there was Aira—hanging on to the edge, holding a purple key.

Emily and Naida pulled her back inside, and she directed the pegasi to head back up into the air, just in time. They all hugged, relieved and happy.

"We have all four keys!" Emily cheered. They had done it. All that was left was finding the portal. Could it get her home?

There was only one way to find out. She announced, "To the castle!"

Chapter 9

The Castle

As they soared through the sky, Emily felt energized. Her heart was full with everything she had experienced in Elvendale, and she hoped that she would soon be back in her own world.

Once she got home, she'd miss her new friends, of course. Would she ever see the elves again? She thought of the owl that she'd followed into Elvendale, and wondered if any of the animals her friends could talk to, like Pluma or Miss Spry, could pass through the portal, too. Maybe they could bring messages back and forth, and she could be pen pals with the elves . . .

"Whoa." Aira slowed the pegasi, causing Emily to look up. There on the horizon, rising through the mist, was a dark, mysterious stone structure.

Was this the castle? The gray walls were dirty and crumbling. Wild vines had grown to the tops of the towers. Thick bushes with sharp, pointed thorns covered the ground. There was a moat, but it held only a trickle of dirty water.

"It looks sad," Emily said as they landed lightly near the fortress.

"Look at all those vines and bushes," Naida remarked. "Will we be able to get past them?"

"Yep," Farran said with confidence. He stood in the sleigh and raised his hands to work his magic, then turned to them and said, "Something is happening—my magic is surging! I feel supercharged! Check this out." With a flick of his wrist, the vines and bushes began to move.

"We'll call you Fantastic Farran," Azari said, cheering him on.

"Ferocious Farran," Farran corrected with a dramatic growl.

Under Farran's new power, the ground beneath them rumbled. Was this what an earthquake felt like? Emily was a little scared.

Even though Farran's magic was strong, the plants seemed to be resisting him. Emily could practically feel them shouting, "Go away! You aren't welcome here!"

"Someone used some serious magic to make it hard for anyone to get in!" Farran cried.

Finally, with a resounding crash, the vines gave way, revealing an arched entryway.

"Awesome job!" Aira said.

"I've gotta say . . . Not bad, Ferocious," Azari said, giving Farran a friendly smack on the back.

While the others joked, Emily seemed to be the only one with a sense of foreboding. The entryway looked dark and unfriendly. There were torches along the way, but untended, they gave off mere glints of light, heavy with smoke.

Emily could tell the pegasi sensed whatever danger she did—they seemed eager to leave. As soon as Aira unhooked the reins, the pegasi took off into the sky.

The group walked through the entrance and down a passage lit with a lone dim torch. Azari used her magic power to take and enhance a ball of fire from the torch to illuminate their path.

Naida said, "It's odd, but I am feeling the same as Farran did—that my magic is somehow much more powerful. And I have a strong feeling that we should go this way . . ." She led them down a hall until a gigantic waterfall blocked their path. The water was black, full of dirt and soot. Naida closed her eyes and twisted her wrist—and the water changed to a brilliant, sparkling blue! She waved her arms and created an opening for them all to pass through.

"Wow," Emily said softly to herself. When the water changed color, the castle seemed a little brighter. Just a tiny bit, but Emily could feel it.

Around the next corner, they encountered a wide lava flow.

"Got it," Azari said. She started using her magic, and also noticed that she was stronger. This time, she could easily part the lava flow so they could all pass. "Piece of Johnny's cake!" Azari said.

Past the lava was a staircase that led them up and up into a dimly lit cavernous room. Shadows danced across the walls.

Suddenly, something rustled up ahead.

Aira shrieked, but Azari said, "Don't be afraid. It's another pegasus!"

"That doesn't mean this one is as nice as the others," Naida said.

"True," Farran said. "Every family has a bad apple." He quickly added, "Not mine, of course . . ."

Aira took a deep breath. "Actually, I am feel-ing supermagic right now, too!" she said. With confidence, Aira slowly approached the creature and bowed low.

Everyone waited in frozen silence. Finally, the pegasus bowed back to Aira.

"This is Golden Glow!" Aira told them at last. "He says he knows where we need to go and he'll lead us there."

That was great news!

Emily's nerves settled as they followed Golden Glow. The castle didn't seem as scary now that they had a leader who knew the way.

He took them up more stairs, through crumbling doorways, and into a huge room, bigger even than the one where they'd found him. Emily thought that Grandmother's whole house could probably have fit into this room.

Then she realized the room wasn't empty. There was a large black throne tucked tightly in the shadows against the back wall. Golden Glow walked over to it.

Azari was the first to follow the pegasus. She revived a dying torch, revealing four small key-holes in a wall near the chair. "That must be how we open the portal," she said, holding her key up.

"We did it!" Aira cheered. She, Naida, and Farran got their keys out as well, and Emily felt a rush of love for her new friends. They'd done this together. And in a few minutes, she'd be home again.

A rustling sound made them all freeze.

"Um, was that Golden Glow?" Farran hissed.

"Azari, can you make it brighter in here?" Emily whispered. "I think somebody's in that throne!"

Emily squinted as Azari raised the fire on the wall torch, casting away the shadows to reveal a woman, tall and thin, dressed in a dusty white and purple robe. She was staring at them with a clouded expression.

In the glow of Azari's flame, Emily could see the woman's eyes were rimmed in red, with dark circles below them. This must be where the castle's sadness came from. This woman, whoever she was, had so much sorrow the entire mountaintop shared it with her.

The woman's eyes widened. "You are not welcome here," she said. Golden Glow whinnied. "Leave now, or face the consequences."

"We've come so far . . ." Emily said in a cracked voice. She could see the keyholes. They had the keys. "Please," she asked, "who are you?"

"I am Skyra, Guardian of the Portal," the

woman announced in a low whisper that echoed eerily through the room. "How did you get here?" she demanded.

Naida reluctantly held up the map.

"Where did you get that?" Skyra's voice boomed through the cavernous space. "There has never been a map to the portal."

Farran sucked in his gut and said bravely, "Well . . . we have one . . ."

"But who made it?!" Skyra stomped her foot on the stone floor. The elves and Emily looked at one another uneasily. "No matter," Skyra continued. "You've come this far. But to open the portal, you need more than just those keys. Go back to where you started because I will *never* let you pass!"

The word *never* echoed over and over. Emily felt the sorrow of the atmosphere beginning to overtake her, but she couldn't get discouraged now!

"Madame Guardian," she said, bravely stepping forward. "We don't mean to disturb you—"

"Silence!" Skyra pounded a tall walking staff, making the floor quake. "That portal was built for one special person. Now she is gone, and it will never be used again!"

"I need to go through it!" Emily wailed. Skyra looked at her stonily. Emily turned and walked a few steps away, and her friends gathered around her.

"What should we do now?" Azari asked.

"Well, we actually haven't followed the map's last instruction," Naida reminded them. "Emily's clue."

"That's right!" Emily grabbed the map, and it shimmered. The message that had appeared

for her before when they first started out—
which felt so long ago—appeared again. She
read, *"Greetings, Four Elements and Girl from
Another World. You will need each other to claim the
legacy of the sisters."*

"Oh!" Aira said, catching on. "We worked
together, but now we have to *'claim the legacy of
the sisters!'* "

"But we aren't sisters," Farran said. "Plus, in
case you forgot, I'm a boy!"

"You're like a sister to me," Azari said with a
laugh. "And there are five of us. In the legend,
the sisters opened the portal with the keys. So
that's what we have to do!"

"Are you forgetting the Queen of Mean?"
Farran asked. Imitating Skyra's voice, he said,
"NEVER!"

"What was that?!" Skyra shouted angrily.

"Er . . . nothing," Farran replied guiltily.

"Finding all the keys also seemed impossible at first," Emily said. "But we always found a way!"

"So what's the plan?" Farran said.

"No plan," Azari said. "Action!" She rushed toward the throne, catching Skyra off guard. The other elves were right behind her, all using their magic any way they could think of. Skyra raised her staff and a gust of wind blew Azari's small fireball into a gigantic flame. The elves zigzagged across the room, dodging the fire.

Azari used her magic to sweep the flames together into one area, and Naida called up water from the moat to extinguish the blaze.

Then Skyra conjured a mighty hurricane wind, but Aira was able to turn it into a tiny harmless breeze.

Skyra's wind encouraged wild vines to curl in through the windows like snakes, threatening to attack them, but Farran cut off the ends and turned them into a bouquet, while Azari's fire caused the vines to shrivel back.

Emily hung back, shouting, "Farran! To your left!" and "Azari—duck!"

One by one, each elf reached the wall to thrust their key into the corresponding keyhole and turn it.

Finally, the fourth key was in . . . but the portal didn't open.

"I told you," Skyra said. "The keys aren't enough!"

All the magic fighting stopped.

Emily was devastated. Her sorrow mingled with Skyra's, and the castle seemed darker than ever. The portal wasn't open. She had lost all hope. She was going to be in Elvendale forever.

The elves gathered around Emily, holding her tight as they walked toward the door.

Chapter 10

The Portal

Emily couldn't believe it was going to end this way. Her chest was tight and her tears flowed freely.

Before they left the room, Emily turned back and took one last look at Skyra. The Guardian sat with her head hung low, taking heavy breaths.

Suddenly, Emily knew what to do.

"I think Skyra is doing this to us because

she's filled with so much sorrow she can't bear to see anyone else happy. She's heartbroken," Emily said. Thinking of the love she still felt for her grandmother, she continued, "I know exactly how that feels. It's endless sadness. Your heart feels shattered into a zillion pieces, and you don't think it can be mended." She touched the cool medallion around her neck.

"How do you heal a broken heart?" Farran asked. "I can fix things, but nothing that would help now."

"I can invent things," Aira said. "But this is bigger than my talents, too."

"I . . ." Emily thought about her walk in Grandmother's garden. She'd gone there to make her own heart feel better. Now that she had had this adventure, and had shared

Grandmother's song and some of her stories with new friends on the way, she realized she did feel better. "Let me try."

Emily approached the throne. "Skyra, I understand what it's like to lose someone you love. It hurts in a way you didn't think was possible. But maybe if you help us, your heart will begin to heal."

Skyra turned her head away, but Emily could tell she was still listening.

"You feel like you'll be lonely forever, right? Like it'll always be this bad." She took the chain from around her neck and held it up so the blue pendant caught a tiny ray of light that streamed in from a crumbled window.

"My grandmother gave me this medallion to keep her close in my heart," Emily said quietly.

She took the necklace off and looked at the stone on her palm. Skyra raised her head, and Emily nearly dropped the pendant as the stone became a bright, glimmering blue—just as it had when she'd first come through the portal to Elvendale.

What was even more shocking was that the top of Skyra's staff also began to glow the same blue.

Emily stared at the staff. Skyra stared at the medallion.

Tipping her head, eyes filled with confusion, Skyra began to sing softly . . .

"Earth moves the air,
And the wind feeds the fire.
Magic is here,
If you dare to believe . . ."

Emily joined in for the next verse, their voices getting louder and stronger as they sang together.

"Sail out to sea
On an ocean of mystery,
And bring your heart
To the ones that you meet."

Suddenly, the sorrow that coated the castle lifted. A burst of magic came from Skyra's staff. The walls repaired themselves, and light filled the room. Fresh air blew in through the little windows, clearing the dust and dirt. Flowers bloomed from vines that crept in through the windows and now decorated the walls. A rainbow arched across the center of the room.

"How do you know that song?" Emily asked Skyra.

"It is the song of the five sisters," Skyra replied. Emily noticed how beautiful she was now that her sadness had been swept away. Skyra looked closely at Emily, really seeing her for the first time. She smiled at Emily's ears. "I know who you are!"

"You do?" Emily asked, completely shocked.

"Yes," Skyra answered, looking a little shocked herself. "If I am right, your grand-mother was the fifth sister in the legend."

The air felt suddenly thick. Emily was stunned. "No. That's not possible."

With a thoughtful gaze, Skyra squinted and asked, "Tell me, what is your name?"

"I'm Emily," she replied. "Emily Jones."

Skyra surprised them by laughing happily.

"Of course! Emily Jones, granddaughter of Emily and Richard Jones."

"But . . . how?" As Emily considered this stunning information, the elves gathered around her.

"I never thought this day would come," Skyra said. "Welcome, Emily Jones!"

"So her grandmother was one of the sisters!" Aira whispered to Farran, who replied, "I knew it all along!"

Skyra explained, "She was not an elf, and she struggled to live in this magical world. She had those crazy round ears! She eventually discovered another world full of people like her, but realized that if she stayed there, she would become mortal." Shaking her head, Skyra added, "It was the hardest decision of her entire life, and she put off making it. But then she met Richard."

"Grandfather?" Emily asked.

"Yes. She fell in love and followed her heart to him." Skyra touched her own heart and said, "Though she did not have any magic, your grandmother had the greatest gift of all."

"I don't understand," Emily said. "What was her gift if it wasn't magic?"

"Her love." Skyra helped Emily hang the medallion back around her neck. "You have shown that same love in your kindness to me, your courage, and your ability to unite these elves of the four elements on this quest."

"It's true!" Naida said. "We all worked together."

Skyra said, "I no longer need to protect the portal from this side. From today forward, you will able to travel back and forth whenever Elvendale calls you. Emily Jones, your love is the final key needed to open the portal."

"My love? Elvendale is going to call?" Emily wasn't sure what that meant. She started to ask. "I—"

"Emily, look," Skyra pointed her staff, and in the center of the room was the portal. It was an oval of swirling blue fog, sparkling and magical. Flickering images of earth, fire, wind, and water mingled together in the mist. "The portal is open to you now," Skyra said. "Your home is waiting."

"I need to say good-bye," Emily said, feeling like she wanted to leave and wanted to stay at the same time.

The elves clearly felt as conflicted as Emily.

"We know you have to go, but we wish you could stay in Elvendale!" Azari said.

Emily replied, "Thank you all for your amazing kindness. I'll never forget it."

Aira leapt forward and hugged Emily tight. "That's right, you won't! Because this isn't good-bye. It's more like 'see ya.'"

Naida and Azari jumped in with more hugs. "We love you!"

Farran wrapped his arms around all the girls. "I knew you were special when I saw those ears!"

"Our not-an-elf," Azari said, just as she had when they first met. "Little Ears Emily."

Everyone laughed.

"Now, my dear," Skyra told Emily, escorting her to the edge of the mist. "One more thing. You must not tell anyone about the portal. Elvendale is a special place, and we need to keep it safe."

"Of course." Emily nodded. She desperately wanted to protect her new friends and all of Elvendale.

Suddenly, an owl fluttered into the castle. A white owl with a golden markings on his chest! He settled on the edge of Skyra's throne and watched.

Golden Glow whinnied from the corner, and bowed low toward Emily.

"You know what to do." Skyra said with a warm smile. "The heart knows the way . . ."

Emily ran into Grandmother's house shouting, "I'm back!"

"Oh, good," her mother said. "We were just finishing up here. Ready to go?"

"What?" Emily said. "But I've been gone for so long! I thought you'd be worried."

Her father looked at his watch and chuckled. "It's only been twenty minutes! You and your imagination . . ."

"But . . ."

Emily looked at her parents. Her journey had really happened! But, here, in her world, it was as if no time had passed at all.

She wished she could tell her parents about her adventures. She'd sailed across the sea in a boat, met a squirrel, eaten at a bakery at the base of an active volcano, and flown through the sky with two pegasi. She'd made wonderful new friends, experienced lots of magic, and helped solve clues to help get her home. And she'd met Skyra, who missed Grandmother as much as she did . . .

But Emily had promised Skyra she wouldn't tell anyone. And, honestly, she doubted her parents would believe her, anyway.

"We have something to ask you," her mother cut in to her thoughts. "It's important."

Emily held her breath. What could it be? Did they somehow know about Elvendale?

"We were wondering," her father said. "How would you like to live here? We know how much you love the garden. If you'd like, we can all move into Grandmother's house. It'll become ours."

Emily jumped up and wrapped her arms around her parents. "I'd love it!" She glanced over their shoulders into the garden, toward the tree where she'd gone through the portal.

"Wow," her mom said. "We didn't know you'd be so excited."

"I am!" Emily said. "Can we stay here tonight?"

"Of course," her father told her. "Why don't you go get washed up for dinner." He looked down at her tennis shoes and shook his head. "Those things sure are dirty!"

Emily laughed. She ran to the room that was now hers, and sat on the bed.

"Whoa!" She leapt up and turned around. The abstract painting hanging over her bed actually depicted four keys! In all the nights she'd slept in this room visiting Grandmother, she'd never noticed. As she looked closer at the overlapping keys, she saw that behind one key was a cloud; behind another, flames; behind the third, a tree; and behind the fourth, a wave.

Emily was shocked. She'd always thought the painting was just some crazy modern art that Grandmother had picked up at a flea market. Now she wondered if maybe Grandmother had painted it herself.

"I love you, Grandmother," she said out loud. She sat on the bed, and felt something lumpy in